No Books on the Shelf

Sandy Fuller Savage

WestBow Press books may be ordered through booksellers or by contacting:

WestBow Press
A Division of Thomas Nelson & Zondervan
1663 Liberty Drive
Bloomington, IN 47403
www.westbowpress.com
844-714-3454

Interior Image Credit: Kateryna Rohotova

ISBN: 978-1-6642-3688-2 (sc)
ISBN: 978-1-6642-3690-5 (hc)
ISBN: 978-1-6642-3689-9 (e)

Library of Congress Control Number: 2021911624

Print information available on the last page.

WestBow Press rev. date: 6/30/2021

WESTBOW
PRESS®
A DIVISION OF THOMAS NELSON
& ZONDERVAN

No Books on the Shelf

It all started with a dream....

One night, I dreamed I was waking up to a very bright, sunny morning. I had started reading a book the night before, and I couldn't wait to read more!

As I opened my sleepy morning eyes and looked toward the bookcase, I realized the bookshelf was there, but all of my books were gone!

All of the books had all been replaced by trinkets, picture frames, toys, and special dolls I didn't even play with. I blinked my eyes furiously—one, two, then five times—to make sure what I saw was correct.

"No books! Where are my books?"
I said in a loud voice.

When Mom heard me yelling, she came to my bedroom door and asked what was happening.

"Mom, where are all of my books? What has happened to them? They are all gone!"

"Oh, Charlotte, don't you remember. Your books have been gone for a long time. We started giving them away little by little years ago. You said you didn't care to read them anymore since you had your new computer," Mom said.

"You told us you didn't need books anymore because you could read any book you wanted on your computer, so we got rid of all the books on the shelf."

Disbelieving I would have done such a thing, I asked Mom if she would take me to the library. After a long pause, she agreed hesitantly and said I might be surprised at what I would find.

Not understanding why she didn't want to take me to the library, I continued to get ready for our "field trip."

We headed downtown to the beautiful library on the town square. I first visited the library when I was a small, young girl. Mom and Dad always told me that reading opened up a whole new world for you to know about. Through reading books, I began to see the world and all different types of people, traditions, and cultures that make up the world.

When we arrived at the library, we got out of the car and walked up the 10 big, tall steps to the front doors. I knew there were 10 because I always counted them as I walked up! At the top, we opened the big, tall doors. When I opened them, I realized that they were not as heavy as I had remembered. I think that's because I am getting older and stronger and even smarter!

Then, I looked into library through
the door window, and I saw something
I would have never believed.

There were no books on the shelves!
Mom immediately saw my face and
knew what I was thinking.

"Charlotte, life is different now. We are in a new era now, and everything has changed! We can hold hundreds of books in our hands at one time with modern technology!"

I just couldn't believe what I was seeing. "A world without tangible books...how sad," I thought as my eyes began to fill with tears.

Then, out of nowhere, a loud noise woke me!

I sat up in my bed and frantically
looked around the room.

My eyes focused on something special—
my books. They were all right there on
the shelf! Right where they belong.

Oh, my goodness, I had been dreaming!
Boy was I happy it was just a dream!

I ran over and hugged my bookshelf!

Then, I sat down, took out a book, and stared at it. I thought about what Mom said in my dream—things change! Life is always changing, but for now, I'm going to enjoy all my books on the shelf!

Lightning Source UK Ltd.
Milton Keynes UK
UKHW050248060721
386671UK00007B/235